Scream School

Look for more books in the Goosebumps Series 2000
by R.L. Stine:

Scream School

AN
APPLE
PAPERBACK

SCHOLASTIC INC.
New York Toronto London Auckland
Sydney New Delhi Hong Kong

A PARACHUTE PRESS BOOK

ISBN-13: 978-0-590-68519-1

This edition is for sale in Indian subcontinent only.

First Scholastic printing, March 1999
Reprinted by Scholastic India Pvt. Ltd., September 2007
March 2008; January; August 2010; May 2011; January 2012
July; December 2013; September; December 2014; July
December 2015

Printed at JJ Offset Printers, Noida

1

"We shouldn't be here, Rita," Ron whispered. The yellow beam of light from his flashlight bounced over the shaggy, worn carpet in front of them.

"I know," Rita whispered back. "But we're here, right? So we might as well explore." She shook her flashlight, hoping to make it brighter.

A strand of Rita's dark hair fell over her eyes. She brushed it back with her free hand and moved closer to Ron.

A creaking sound made them both gasp. The circles of light swept the cracked plaster on the walls, then washed over the furniture covered in dusty sheets.

"Just the old house settling," Ron whispered, swallowing hard. "Old houses do that, you know. Settle."

1

"I thought that only happened in dumb horror movies," Rita replied. She picked up the edge of a sheet and squinted at the arm of a big couch.

"Wish we were at the movies," Ron murmured, unable to keep his voice from trembling. A shudder ran down his long, lean body. He tugged off his baseball cap and mopped his forehead with his shirtsleeve.

"If you're so scared, why did you dare me to come here?" Rita snapped. Her green eyes flashed in the dim, darting light.

"I didn't dare you," Ron protested. "You dared me."

"No. You," Rita insisted. "Don't you remember? We were walking home from school. And you said you were sick and tired of everyone calling our school *Scream School*."

"Yeah, but —"

"You said everyone in town laughs at us because we're always being terrified by ghouls and monsters and gruesome creeps. Kids at our school are always screaming their heads off. And that's why everyone calls it Scream School. And —"

"Yes, I said that," Ron interrupted. "But I didn't —"

"And then you said you weren't the tiniest bit scared of Johnny Scream. You said you didn't care how many kids that ugly dead ghoul has murdered. You said you would break right into his house — the house where he died fifty years ago. And then you dared me to come with you."

Rita raised the light to Ron's face. She held it there until he covered his eyes and turned away.

"Okay, okay. I remember. I said that," he told her. "So here we are. This is where that creep lives. We broke in. Now what?"

"You tell me," Rita replied, brushing her dark hair off her face again. "It was your big idea."

"Well . . ." Ron hesitated as another creaking noise made them spin around.

No one there.

"We've done it," Ron said softly. "We've proven we're not afraid of Johnny Scream, right?"

Rita nodded. "I guess."

"So let's go home."

She didn't argue with him. Her legs were trembling as she followed him through the dark, cluttered room to the front door. She hoped Ron couldn't see how frightened she was.

Ron let out a little squeak as he tugged the knob on the front door. He tugged it again. Harder.

"Wh-what's wrong?" Rita stammered. She stumbled and bumped him from behind.

"The door —" he moaned. "It's . . . locked."

"Locked from the outside? That's impossible!" she cried. "It can't be locked. It must be stuck."

She set her flashlight on the floor. Shoved him aside. And gripped the doorknob with both hands.

Rita tugged with all her might, groaning as she twisted the brass knob and pulled.

"We came in through this door," she gasped. "So it can't be locked."

Ron handed her his flashlight. Sweat poured down his forehead, into his eyes. He ignored it and tried the door again.

"There's no one here. So who could have locked the door?"

"How do you know there's no one here? Maybe Johnny Scream . . ."

"Shut up! Don't be funny! Just get us out of here! Hurry!"

Struggling breathlessly with the door, their panic growing with every second, the two teenagers didn't hear the creak of floorboards across the darkened living room.

Didn't see the hunched figure lurch toward them.

Didn't hear his low grunts with each heavy, plodding step. "*Hunnh hunnh hunnh.*"

Huddled together, twisting the knob, tugging, Ron and Rita didn't see the ghastly creature move behind them. Didn't hear the whoosh of cold air as he swung his axe up onto his shoulder.

And then raised the axe above his head.

They didn't hear his excited wheezing. They didn't see the gleeful grin on the ghoul's twisted face.

Behind the two frantic teens, the axe rose high.

4

And then it started down.

"YAAAAAAIII!"

A shrill scream burst from outside the room.

They all heard a *CRASH*, then a heavy, solid *THUD*.

The ghoul spun around quickly. "Helll-lo!" he called. "Was that in the script? I don't think so!"

UT! CUT!" Emory Banyon cried angrily.

Jake Banyon saw his father jump out of his director's chair. Sprawled on his stomach on the studio floor, Jake struggled to climb to his feet. But he was tangled in the canvas chair that had collapsed beneath him.

"What happened, Emory?" the actress playing Rita called from the set. "That was such a good take."

"I know, I know." Jake's dad groaned. "I guess it was too good. You scared my son right out of his chair!"

Jake heard laughter all around the movie set.

He sighed to himself. This isn't fair, he thought. It wasn't my fault.

Jake knew he was blushing. Everyone was staring at him. Everyone hated him. He had ruined a really good take in his father's new movie.

He could see his friend Chelsea Paige shaking her head.

She must think I'm a total geek, he thought miserably. Look at her. She's pretending she doesn't know me.

"Are we going to break for lunch, or what?" the ghoul called impatiently, dropping his axe to the floor. It bounced across the set. The axe was light, made of balsa wood.

"No. We don't have time," Emory Banyon told him. "You want to spend another three hours in makeup? Let's get the scene, Carl. Then we'll break for lunch."

All three actors grumbled. Carl, the guy playing the ghoul, trudged off to the side to have his makeup repaired.

Emory bent and pulled the chair away so that Jake could stand up. "Jake," he said sternly, lowering his bushy black eyebrows until they came together, "if you're too scared to watch, maybe you should wait outside."

"But I wasn't scared!" Jake protested. "Really. I was enjoying it. It didn't scare me, Emory!"

Jake's dad insisted that *everyone* call him by his first name. Even Jake.

Jake would rather call him *Dad*. But Emory wouldn't allow it.

"You and I are closer than father and son,

right?" he always boomed. "We're *pals*! And pals call each other by their first names."

"Right, Emory," Jake had to agree.

Emory never talked in a quiet voice — he only boomed, as if he were onstage in an opera. With his wild black hair that was never brushed, his bushy eyebrows, his flashing black eyes, his booming, deep voice, Emory attracted attention everywhere he went.

He thought fast. He talked fast. He never walked — he always trotted. He always appeared to be in a hurry. He always seemed to be doing six things at once, giving instructions to a dozen people, talking rapidly into his cell phone, writing frantic notes at the same time.

Sometimes Jake felt slow as a turtle next to his famous movie director father. Sometimes Jake felt as if he lived with a *hurricane*!

"But I wasn't scared of that scene!" Jake protested again. "The dumb chair collapsed, and I fell. It wasn't my fault, Emory."

Emory *tsk-tsked*. He patted Jake's slender shoulder. "It's okay to admit you were scared, son," he replied. "It was a very scary scene. Millions of people will scream when they see it."

"But I only screamed because the chair fell!" Jake cried. He didn't mean for that shrill, whiny voice to come out. But he couldn't stop it. "I wasn't scared, Emory. Really!"

Emory turned to Chelsea. She was still perched

in her tall red canvas chair. Chelsea was twelve, the same age as Jake, pretty with brown eyes and light brown hair streaked with blond.

She wore a red cut-off T-shirt, baggy khaki shorts, and had about a dozen plastic bracelets up and down her right arm.

Chelsea's father also worked in movies. But Jake wasn't sure exactly what he did. Something to do with the business side of things.

Jake only knew that Chelsea wasn't forced to call her dad by his first name. And Mr. Paige didn't make horror movies. So he was never accusing Chelsea of being a chicken and a scaredy-cat all the time.

"Chelsea, there's a ton of food over there," Emory said, pointing to the studio door. "All kinds of sandwiches and salads. Why don't you take Jake and go check it out?"

He didn't wait for Chelsea to reply. He frowned at Jake. Then he swung back to the set and shouted, "Places! Come on. We almost had it. Lights. Cut the lights. Quiet, everyone. Let's go again."

Jake followed Chelsea out the studio door into the hall. He didn't like the smile on Chelsea's face. Was she still laughing at him?

"It wasn't my fault," he told her. "The chair just fell. So don't laugh."

She laughed. "Sorry. But it's kind of funny. They should keep it in the movie."

9

"Ha-ha," Jake replied bitterly.

They stopped in front of the food tables. Chelsea's expression turned serious. Her eyes softened to a warm, sympathetic gaze.

That's what Jake liked about her. She was nice. She didn't just want to show you how much better she was than you.

A lot of kids in Hollywood were very competitive.

"So is it totally awful having such a famous father?" she asked. "Aren't there any good parts to being the son of the *King of Horror*?"

"I can't think of any," Jake moaned. He picked up half a turkey sandwich and dropped it onto a paper plate. He thought hard. "Well . . . I do get into the movies for free. That's pretty cool," he admitted.

"But so does just about everyone else at our school," he added. "So I guess it's no big deal."

He thought some more. "Famous people come to our house all the time. That's a little cool."

He dropped a handful of nacho chips onto his plate. "But the hard part is that everybody always asks me the same question. 'Are you scared of your father's movies? Are you scared of your father's movies?' Over and over. The same dumb question."

Chelsea chewed on a carrot stick. "Can I ask you a serious question?" she asked.

"Yeah. What?" Jake replied.

"Are you scared of your father's movies?"

Chelsea burst out laughing.

Jake slugged her on the arm. Then he raised both hands to her throat and pretended to strangle her.

Still laughing, she tried to jam the carrot stick into his nose.

"It's a good question," Chelsea insisted. "I mean, what else are people going to ask you? Your dad is the King of Horror. So . . ."

"I'm just as scary as he is!" Jake proclaimed. "But he won't believe me. He thinks I get scared all the time. You know why he brings me to his movie set? To show me that the horror isn't real. To teach me not to be afraid."

Jake sighed. "But I'm *not* afraid!" he cried. "I'm not! *Nothing* scares me!"

Jake felt a tap on his shoulder.

He spun around.

Stared.

And opened his mouth in a scream of terror.

ake and Chelsea both gaped at Johnny Scream, the most famous zombie ghoul in history. As the star of Emory Banyon's *Scream School* movies, Johnny Scream's terrifying face was known around the world.

Seven feet tall, straight and skinny as a skeleton, Johnny Scream stared back at Jake and Chelsea with his cold silver eyes. As if blown by the wind, his thick black hair flew back around his rotting, decaying face.

His grin revealed pointed yellow teeth. A chunk of skin was missing from his left cheek. Gray bone poked out from underneath.

Johnny removed his bony hand from Jake's shoulder. His long yellowed fingernails were curled like a canary's claws.

"Hey, Jake — I didn't mean to scare you,"

Johnny Scream said. He had a surprisingly normal voice, pleasant and soft. "Just wanted to say hi."

"I — I wasn't scared," Jake stammered, feeling his face grow hot. Blushing again.

Why was he such an easy blusher? It was totally embarrassing.

Chelsea narrowed her eyes at him. "You weren't scared?" she teased. "You screamed your head off."

"I know," Jake told her. "I was doing the Official Johnny Scream Scream."

A black-lipped grin spread over Johnny Scream's face.

Chelsea frowned at Jake. "Yeah. For sure," she muttered.

"No. Really," Jake insisted. "That was the Official Fan Club Scream. Everyone does it at movie theaters whenever Johnny Scream comes on."

Jake frowned back at her. "You didn't really think I was scared — did you? I mean, Johnny Scream comes to my house all the time. I've known him since I was a baby."

Chelsea rolled her big brown eyes. "Okay, you weren't scared. Like I'll believe anything."

Johnny Scream pawed over the sandwiches. "I've got to get back on the set or your dad will kill me. Do you see any roast beef sandwiches?" he asked Jake. "Can you pick one up for me? Know how hard it is to eat with these stupid curled fingernails?"

*　　*　　*

After the day's shooting, Emory drove Jake and Chelsea to the Banyons' mansion in Beverly Hills. Jake liked showing off his dad's enormous black Mercedes.

"Yes, it's great. My dad has the same car," Chelsea told him. "But I like our new little Volkswagen bug better. It's so cute!"

Jake invited Chelsea to stay for dinner. But when the dinner conversation started, he was sorry he had invited her.

"What's on the menu tonight, Vicki?" Emory asked his wife, giving her a kiss on the cheek.

Jake's mother was a tiny sparrow of a woman, sharp-featured but pretty, with short, smooth blond hair streaked with platinum, and tiny, round blue eyes that beamed onto you like lasers.

She had been a model and had appeared in a few TV commercials before Jake was born. But when Emory's movies became popular and he became the King of Horror, she gave up her career.

"We're having take-out chicken and potato salad," Vicki Banyon announced. "I didn't have time to cook tonight."

"Chicken for a chicken, huh, Jake?" Emory laughed.

"Let's eat." Jake dragged Chelsea into the dining room before his father could crack another dumb joke.

14

Everyone sat down and passed around the bucket of chicken and the potato salad.

"How did it go on the set?" Jake's mom asked Jake.

"Fine," Jake replied.

"I really enjoyed it," Chelsea said, pulling the skin off a chicken breast.

Emory chuckled. "We had a good day — until Jake lost it."

Jake's mom turned her laser eyes on Jake.

"I didn't lose it!" he protested.

"I guess the scene was a good one," Emory continued, grinning. "Jake got so scared, he fell off his chair!"

"Not true!" Jake shrieked. He jumped angrily to his feet. "It's *not true!*"

Chelsea was laughing.

Wasn't she supposed to be his friend?

"Jake, sit down," his mom said softly. "Where's your sense of humor?"

Scowling, Jake dropped back into his seat.

"There's nothing wrong with being scared," Emory said, fumbling around in the bucket, then pulling out a chicken leg. "Most people *like* to be scared — thank goodness!"

"But I wasn't scared —" Jake started.

Emory shoved the bucket across the table to him. "Here. Take some chicken."

Jake reached out both hands and pulled over the cardboard bucket.

"I enjoyed meeting Johnny Scream," Chelsea said. "He seems like a really cool guy."

"He's talented too," Emory said, his eyes on Jake.

Jake tilted the bucket toward him. Started to reach in.

And gasped when he saw the eyeball staring up at him.

A wet yellowish eyeball with tiny red veins stretching over it.

Emory burst out laughing. He gleefully slapped the table with both hands. "Gotcha!" he boomed.

"Emory —" Jake started.

"Did you see the look on his face?" Emory bellowed. "He was terrified!"

Chelsea laughed again.

Mrs. Banyon shook her head.

"Emory, I — I wasn't scared," Jake stammered. "You've done this lame eyeball trick a thousand times before."

Emory tossed back his head, laughing.

Jake picked up the eyeball and threatened to heave it at his father.

Jake's mom snatched the glass eyeball from his hand. She glared at her husband. "Emory, why do you keep trying to scare Jake?" she demanded sharply. "Why do you do it? Just to prove that you're the King of Horror?"

Emory cut off his laughter. His expression

turned serious. "That's not why I do it. Of course not," he insisted.

"Then why?" Jake's mom asked.

"I want Jake to be able to admit when he's scared," Emory replied. "It isn't healthy to do what he always does. It isn't healthy to hold your true feelings in."

"But I *don't!*" Jake insisted shrilly. He balled his hands into tight fists. "I don't! I don't!"

"You know what scares me?" Chelsea chimed in. "The fact that I *never* get scared. I'm not afraid of the dark. Or afraid of movies. Or nightmares. Or *anything.* Sometimes I wonder if that's normal."

"Let's change the subject," Mrs. Banyon said, seeing Jake's tight, angry scowl. "Let's talk about the Dodgers. You're going to the game Saturday, right, Jake?"

Jake nodded, but he didn't reply.

He was thinking. Thinking hard.

How can I prove to my dad that I'm not afraid? he asked himself, glaring across the table as Emory hungrily gobbled down chicken.

I know, he thought. I'll prove that I'm just as scary as he is.

But how?

ake dribbled the ball past his friend Carlos Manza. He gave Carlos a little shove as he went by. Moved to the basket for an easy layup.

And missed.

The ball bounced off the backboard into Carlos's hands. Carlos laughed. "Nice shot."

"I'm just warming up," Jake told him.

Carlos dribbled away, then heaved the ball up from halfway across the court. The ball missed the basket. Missed the backboard. Missed everything.

They watched it bounce across the lawn toward the Banyons' swimming pool.

"I'm just warming up too," Carlos said, laughing.

Carlos was shorter than Jake, but bulky and athletic-looking. He had short black hair, buzz-cut on the sides, spiky on top.

His dark eyes crinkled at the edges. He always appeared to be laughing at something.

He wore baggy shorts and an enormous red T-shirt that came down nearly to his knees. His white high-top sneakers were new. They glowed in the sunlight.

Jake took the ball. Faked one way. Faked the other way. Started to dribble up the middle — and Carlos slapped the ball out of his hands.

They were playing one-on-one in Jake's backyard, on the tennis court that Emory had converted to a basketball court.

Emory told everyone how he grew up on the streets of New York playing basketball. He and Jake played on the backyard court all the time.

When he played with his father, Jake had to be fast — and careful. Emory played to win. In the heat of the game, he would knock Jake to the ground and run over him to get the last shot at the basket. The two of them always kept at it until they were exhausted and drenched with sweat.

Playing against Carlos was a lot more relaxing. Mainly because Carlos was a fun, easygoing guy. And they both had about the same amount of skill — not much.

"You're coming to my house for dinner, right?" Carlos asked, dribbling at the foul line.

"Yeah. And we'll watch a movie?" Jake asked, bending over to catch his breath.

Carlos nodded. Took his foul shot. It swished through the basket.

Jake loved going over to Carlos's house. His parents had their own screening room with a movie projector and full-size screen. And they had the most amazing collection of old horror movies.

Carlos and Jake loved to watch the classic black-and-white films: *Bride of Frankenstein, The Wolf Man, The Invisible Man.*

The two of them screamed their heads off, even though the old films seemed kind of funny now.

One day, Jake told his dad how much he enjoyed the old horror movies.

"Great old stuff," Emory replied. "If you ever get too scared while you're watching, just remind yourself that it's only a movie."

Jake dribbled the ball past Carlos. Carlos slapped at it and missed. Jake went up for his shot.

"Hey, Jake —" A voice from the driveway.

Jake turned. Missed the shot. The ball hit the rim and bounced away.

Chelsea came running over, her light brown hair flying behind her. She wore a white tennis outfit and carried a tennis racket. "What are you guys doing?" she asked.

"Knitting a sweater," Jake replied. He was still angry that she had laughed at him at dinner the night before. "What does it look like we're doing?"

Chelsea pretended to hit him on the head with

her tennis racket. "I meant, are you playing a game or just messing around?"

"Both," Carlos replied, grinning. "Want to play? How about Jake and me against you?"

"No way," Chelsea replied. She set her racket down on the grass beside the court. "Basketball isn't my sport. I kind of stink at it."

"Okay. You and Jake against me," Carlos suggested. "I'll try to go easy on you two."

They started their game. Chelsea tried to dribble the ball past Carlos, who danced in front of her, waving both hands in her face.

"Pass it! Pass it!" Jake cried.

Chelsea dribbled to the basket. Shot and scored.

"Lucky shot," Carlos murmured.

He took the ball out. Started to dribble, dancing to one side, then the other. Fancy footwork.

Showing off for Chelsea, Jake thought.

Chelsea moved in front of Carlos — and stole the ball from his hands. She dribbled, backing over the half-court line, then moving forward.

"Pass it! Here!" Jake called, waving his arms over his head. "I'm open!"

Chelsea ignored him and fired off a two-handed layup. It swished through the basket. "Four to zip," she told Carlos.

"Hey — am I in this game or what?" Jake complained.

"Know what Jake did yesterday on his dad's

movie set?" Chelsea asked Carlos. She cast a mischievous, teasing glance at Jake.

"No, what?" Carlos asked, dribbling in place.

"Shut up, Chelsea!" Jake snapped. "Just shut up!"

"What did he do?" Carlos asked, grinning at Chelsea.

Chelsea opened her mouth to reply.

But all three of them froze when they heard the loud growls. And saw the enormous black rottweiler come roaring into the yard.

The ball fell out of Carlos's hands and rolled away.

"Oh, no . . . I know this dog," Jake moaned, backing up.

Barking furiously, the huge dog lowered its head, preparing to attack.

"No, Dukie! No!" Jake pleaded. He raised both hands, trying to shield himself. "Dukie — down! Down!"

The dog opened its jaws in a furious growl.

"Oh . . . help!" Jake cried as the dog raised its front paws. Leaped heavily onto him. Knocked Jake to the ground.

And lowered its massive head to attack.

ukie — no! Nooooo!" Jake howled.

But the dog stood over Jake, its big paws pressing Jake's shoulders to the ground. It lowered its head. And licked.

Licked . . .

"Dukie — stop! Dukie!" Jake pleaded.

The dog licked Jake's face . . . licked his neck. Its stubby tail wagged furiously.

In seconds, Jake's cheeks and neck were glistening ···ith wet dog slime.

"Pull him off!" Jake begged his friends. "He does this to me all the time. He thinks he's still a puppy. Owww! He weighs a *ton*! Owww! Dukie — you're *crushing* me!"

Chelsea and Carlos looked on helplessly.

Dukie finally got tired of giving Jake a tongue

bath. He backed off, panting, his tail twirling like a propeller.

Jake saw his father trotting across the lawn. "Emory?"

Dukie bounded over to greet Mr. Banyon. The dog's tongue trailed from its mouth as it ran.

Emory gave its head a few pats, then dropped beside Jake. "You okay?" he asked.

Jake pulled himself up to a sitting position. He wiped sticky dog saliva off his cheek with the back of one hand. "Yeah. Fine."

Emory's face filled with concern. He placed a hand on Jake's shoulder. "Jake — why didn't you ever tell me that you're scared of dogs?"

Jake squinted up at his father. "Huh?"

"I had no idea," Emory continued, shaking his head. "But don't worry. We can deal with the problem."

"Problem? What problem?" Jake cried.

Chelsea and Carlos watched from the basketball court. Carlos picked up the ball and tossed it from hand to hand.

"The first thing is to admit it," Emory told Jake. "Admit that you're afraid of dogs. Once you realize you have a problem, we can —"

"But I'm *not* — !" Jake protested. "Emory, I just —"

"I saw the whole thing, Jake," Emory replied, patting Jake's shoulder again.

"Dukie is pretty scary," Chelsea chimed in.

"He is *not!*" Jake cried angrily. "I've known him since he was a puppy. And he's just playful, that's all."

Emory climbed to his feet. He reached down and pulled Jake up. "Know what? I'll get you a dog, Jake. Your birthday is coming up. I'll buy you a dog for your birthday. That will help you work out your problems."

"But, Emory — if you'd only listen to me . . ."

"Having your own dog will help you get over your fear."

A phone rang. Emory pulled a cell phone from the pocket of his khakis. He flipped it open and began talking into it as he walked back to the house.

Jake turned to his friends. They both had wide grins on their faces.

"Look out, Jake — the neighbors' cat is over there," Carlos said, pointing.

"We'll protect you," Chelsea teased. "Don't be afraid. We won't let it get you."

Laughing scornfully, they slapped each other a high five.

Jake let out an angry, frustrated cry. He grabbed the basketball — and heaved it as high and as hard as he could.

All three of them watched it sail high into the sky, bounce once on the grass, and then splash into the swimming pool.

"Nice shot," Carlos murmured.

Jake just growled in reply.

That night, Jake stepped out of Carlos's house and began walking home. It was a clear, warm night. A million stars glittered overhead. The light from a full moon made the perfectly trimmed Beverly Hills lawns shimmer like silver.

Jake crossed the street onto the next block. The houses were mostly dark. Streetlamps cast yellow light, making his shadow stretch far in front of him.

A warm breeze brushed against him as he walked. The breeze rustled the low hedges along the sidewalk.

A screech in a tree limb made Jake gaze up. A bird? A cat?

He couldn't see.

To his surprise, the stars had all vanished. He watched a black cloud slide quickly over the moon.

The ground darkened. His shadow faded into the deepening blackness.

So dark now. Suddenly so dark.

Eerily dark.

He crossed the street and stepped into a thick, damp mist. A strange green glow against the darkness. Swirling snakes of green cloud, hovering low against the ground, curling around his ankles.

The thick green fog curling around him, washing over him. Sweeping so silently around him, as if pulling him inside.

Holding him in its green glow. Holding him . . . pressing against him so wetly . . . trapping him.

"Hey —" Jake uttered a strangled cry.

He took another step. His legs suddenly felt as heavy as lead.

"Hey —"

Only two blocks to go until he was home. Why couldn't he see the houses now? What happened to the light from the streetlamps?

He heard a rustling behind the hedge. Footsteps.

"Hey —"

Why couldn't he see the hedge?

The green fog wrapped around him, tightening its grip, so warm and wet.

He couldn't see. Couldn't see anything.

"Hey — hey — what's *happening*?"

ake heard scrambling behind the hedge. A frantic rustling like small animals scampering over leaves.

"I can't see anything," he murmured.

And then the thick green mist appeared to split apart.

And a figure loomed quickly in front of him. A figure of shimmering blue shadows. So tall and thin . . . taller than a human.

And then from out of the shadows, a face. A haunted, distorted face.

And Jake cried out in shock — "Johnny Scream!"

Johnny's silver eyes glared down at Jake, glowing green, reflecting the mist. His black lips curled in a cold smile. He stretched out bony arms as if trying to block Jake's way.

"Wh-what are you doing here?" Jake stammered. "I was walking home, and this weird fog came up, and —"

"You can't go home," Johnny Scream rasped. The curled fingernails clicked on his clenching fists.

"Excuse me?" Jake stared up at the giant ghoul. The green mist swirled around them both, hot and wet.

The street was so silent . . . no cars . . . no voices . . . no rustle of wind in the trees.

Jake could hear his own rapid breathing, hear the thud of his heartbeat in his chest.

"You can't go home, Jake," Johnny Scream repeated, the silver eyes so cold and lifeless.

"Johnny — are you trying to scare me?" Jake asked. His voice sounded tiny, muffled in the choking fog.

Johnny Scream's black suit, patched and torn and many sizes too big, fluttered in the swirling fog, a flapping sound — like a flag in the wind. Or bat wings.

The silver eyes never blinked.

The ghoul's smile revealed two rows of pointed teeth. Sharp spikes.

He clicked the fingernails on his right hand against his fingernails on his left hand in a steady, slow rhythm.

CLICK-CLICK CLICK-CLICK . . . the only sound now except for Jake's shallow breaths.

29

"Johnny — why are you trying to scare me?" Jake demanded. He tried to take a step back. But the fog held him. Pushed against him. Prickled the skin on the back of his neck.

"I'm real, Jake," the ghoul whispered. The patch of cheekbone beneath the open skin glowed green.

"Huh? What are you *saying*?"

"I'm real, Jake. I can't let you go home."

"Johnny, I know you," Jake insisted, unable to keep his voice from trembling. "I know you're not real. You're in my dad's movies."

"I'm not in the movies now," the ghoul replied coldly.

"But you're not real!" Jake declared. "It's all makeup, Johnny. I know it's all makeup!"

With an angry cry, Jake stuck out both hands — and grabbed Johnny Scream's face.

"All makeup!" Jake screamed. And tried to pull off the skin flap. Tried to pull off the ugly mask over the actor's real face.

"Oh!" Jake gasped as his hands stuck to Johnny's face.

His skin was soft — soft and sticky like thick syrup.

Jake tried to tug his fingers free. But they stuck to the soft skin, then stretched it, like taffy, like bubblegum . . .

Jake pulled back — and the sickening, sticky skin kept stretching with him.

I'm stuck! he realized. Stuck to the ghoul's face!

Johnny Scream's eyes gleamed like two beams of light. His black-lipped smile spread, stretched . . . stretched . . .

And Jake, pulling . . . pulling . . . struggling to free his hands from the rubbery skin, opened his mouth in a horrified scream.

s the scream faded, the fog faded with it, leaving a glowing darkness. Jake blinked. He couldn't see the grinning ghoul any longer.

His whole body shook. Shook up and down.

He blinked again — and stared up at his father. Over his dark, sleepy eyes, Emory's bushy eyebrows wriggled like two fat worms.

Jake realized his father had hold of his shoulders and was shaking him. Shaking him out of his dream.

"Wake up, Jake. You're having a nightmare." Emory's normally booming voice was clogged from sleep. He wore baggy, striped pajama bottoms. His bare chest, with its nest of thick black hair, loomed over Jake.

"It's a nightmare," Emory repeated.

Jake sat up slowly. He raised both hands and stared at his fingers, as if expecting them to be sticky from Johnny Scream's face.

"Wow," Jake murmured. "Wow."

"You're okay," Emory said soothingly, letting go of Jake's shoulders. "But that was quite a scream. You probably woke up half of Beverly Hills."

"It was a pretty scary dream," Jake admitted. "I dreamed about Johnny Scream. He wouldn't let me come home, and —"

"So my movie *did* scare you!" Emory cried triumphantly. He jumped to his feet and clasped his big hands together.

"Well . . ." Jake cleared his throat. The bedroom was air-conditioned, but his pajamas were drenched with sweat.

"It's great you can finally admit it, Jake," Emory declared happily. "Don't you feel a *million* times better admitting that you were scared?"

Jake groaned. "Emory, it was just a stupid nightmare. Everyone has nightmares."

"I know it's hard being the son of the King of Horror, Jake," Emory said, scratching his bare chest. "But if you can just face your fear . . . that's the first step."

"But, Emory —"

A smile spread over Emory's face. He squeezed Jake's shoulder again. "I'm proud of you. Very proud."

"*But I'm not scared of your movies!*" Jake shrieked. "Listen to me! I'm *not* scared!"

Emory motioned with both hands for Jake to calm down. "Shhhh. Let's get some sleep. You've had a hard night." He turned and made his way to the bedroom door.

"But, Emory — I *like* scary movies," Jake called after him. "I watch scary movies all the time."

His dad didn't seem to hear. He padded out to the hallway without turning around and vanished into his room.

He only hears what he wants to hear, Jake thought bitterly.

It made Emory so happy that I had a nightmare about Johnny Scream. How can I prove to him that I'm not scared? That I'm as brave as he is?

Through the wall, he could hear his parents talking in their bedroom. They're probably talking about me, Jake thought with a sigh.

Emory is probably telling Mom that I finally admitted what a coward I am. That I finally admitted I'm terrified of the *Scream School* movies.

What am I going to do?

When will I ever have a chance to prove to Emory that I'm not scared?

When?

The next morning, Jake got his chance.

8

Chelsea came over the next morning. She slipped in through the kitchen door as Jake was finishing his Frosted Flakes.

She wore a white tank top over baggy pale blue shorts. Her blue plastic sandals clonked on the tile floor. She sat down across from Jake and poured herself a glass of orange juice.

"What's up?"

"Mmmpf mmmpf," Jake mumbled, with a mouthful of cereal.

"Mom is driving to Westwood this morning," Chelsea reported. "We could go with her and — you know — hang out. Maybe walk around the UCLA campus?"

Jake opened his mouth to reply. But Emory burst into the room, talking loudly into his cell phone. He wore a sleeveless red T-shirt over wrinkled khaki shorts. His unbrushed black hair was wilder than ever, poking straight up on his head.

He lowered the phone from his mouth to talk to Jake and Chelsea. "Want to be in the movie? I need some extras this morning."

Jake and Chelsea exchanged glances.

"What do we have to do?" Jake asked.

"Nothing scary," Emory replied. "It's a classroom scene. I need to fill up the seats. You just sit in art class, that's all."

"Cool!" Chelsea declared.

Jake agreed. "Okay. Count us in!"

As they drove to the studio, Emory explained the scene in a little more detail.

"It's a big art class at *Scream School*. A boy is locked in the supply closet at the back of the room. The kids are making so much noise, they can't hear him pounding on the closet door, trying to get out.

"The kids are all working on art projects. Suddenly, a boy shouts, 'Hey — check out my project!' The kids all look up. The boy has a bunch of big snakes — poisonous snakes — climbing all over the table.

"They look around. And there are snakes everywhere. Snakes on the tables. On the floor. Snakes in the sink. Snakes crawling up the wall. Everyone panics. They all start screaming and running around.

"The boy finally bursts out of the supply closet. He can't believe what he sees. The room has emptied out — and he's surrounded by hissing snakes."

Emory turned the Mercedes into the studio lot. He gave the guard in the little booth a salute and headed toward the parking lot.

"Are the snakes real?" Jake asked.

Emory nodded. "Most of them. But they're not dangerous. They've all been defanged."

He pulled the car into his reserved space. "But you don't have to worry, Jake. You won't be near any snakes."

"I'm not worried," Jake protested.

"What do we have to do?" Chelsea asked.

"You're students in the art class," Emory told her. "You'll be near the back. You just have to pretend to paint or something. No big deal."

Jake and Chelsea had to wait around on the set for nearly two hours. First, the crew had trouble with the lighting in the classroom set. Then Emory discovered that not enough snakes had been delivered. He angrily sent someone to get two dozen more.

Jake and Chelsea hung out with the other extras. They all wanted to ask Jake what it was like to be the King of Horror's son.

"It's great," Jake replied. "Really awesome."

He walked over to the food table to get a bagel

and some juice — and bumped into Devon Klar. Devon had been on a popular TV show about vampire teenagers for a few years. This was his first movie.

"Whoa!" Devon let out a cry of surprise as he studied Jake. "You look like my twin!"

"Huh?" Jake stared hard at Devon.

Devon was right. He was taller than Jake and more muscular. But they both had the same straight brown hair, dark, serious eyes, full mouths, and square jaws.

"You're Emory's son, right?" Devon asked, still studying Jake's features.

Jake nodded.

"What's it like?" Devon asked. "I mean, is he scary at home?"

"Not too," Jake told him.

Devon piled a couple of cherry danishes on a plate. "What are you doing here? Just hanging out?"

"I'm an extra today," Jake said. "You know. In the art class."

"Cool," Devon murmured. "Well . . . have fun, Twin." He walked off with a plate piled high with food.

Jake returned to Chelsea, who was sitting on a wooden crate, reading *People* magazine. "Did you bring me a bagel?" she asked, not looking up from the magazine.

"No. Did you want one?" Jake asked.

"Not really."

"Do you think I look like Devon Klar's twin?" Jake asked.

"In your dreams," Chelsea replied.

"Extras on the set! Extras!" Sheila Farrel, the assistant director, was calling. She was a tall, thin young woman with short red hair that bounced as she walked. "Extras in the classroom. Places."

Jake took a last bite of bagel and followed Chelsea onto the classroom set. He knew his part was easy. Nothing to it. But his heart began to pound anyway.

"Could we have a run-through?" Sheila shouted. "We need to block this."

"Where's Devon?" Emory called. He glanced at Jake as he brushed past him. "Devon? Is he in makeup?"

"Sheila told me I don't need makeup," Devon said, trotting up to Emory. "I'm locked in the closet, right?"

"Right." Emory glanced at the clipboard in his hand. "You're trying to break out. We're only shooting you from behind. No makeup."

Jake and Chelsea followed Sheila to a table near the back of the room. She pointed to paper and paints spread out on the tabletop. "Just paint whatever you want," she instructed them. "It doesn't matter. But concentrate on your paintings — and don't talk to each other."

"No problem," Jake replied. He and Chelsea took their places.

Sheila moved the other extras into place. Devon stepped into the supply closet. A crew member carefully closed the door behind him.

The closet had no ceiling, Jake saw. A camera was perched on the top of the back wall, aimed at Devon's back. A second camera stood at the front of the classroom, ready to film the art students.

"Call the snake wranglers," Emory ordered. "I want the snakes in place for the run-through. But leave them in their cages." He clapped his hands. "Snakes! Bring on the snakes!"

They did three run-throughs before Emory was happy with the scene. Jake and Chelsea dabbed at their paintings, concentrating hard. The snakes writhed and wriggled in their cages. Devon banged on the closet door, pushing, pulling, struggling to get out.

"Okay — let's roll some film," Emory announced. "Let's try a take."

"Quiet!" Sheila screamed. "Quiet, everyone! We're rolling!"

The hammering by the set carpenters across the room stopped. A hush fell over the vast studio.

"Rolling," someone said. "Speed."

And then a loud groan from the supply closet interrupted the silence.

"What was that?" Emory asked, standing beside the camera operator.

Another groan.

And Devon staggered out of the closet, gripping his stomach. "It hurts . . . owww . . . man, it really hurts."

Sheila gasped. Emory set down his clipboard and ran to Devon. "What's wrong? What hurts?"

"My stomach," Devon groaned. "I just ate some danishes. I . . ." His face went totally white. His knees buckled.

Emory grabbed him to keep him from sinking to the floor.

"I think . . . I'm . . . sick. . . ." Devon moaned.

Two crew members helped Devon off. They headed quickly to the back door.

Another loud groan.

"He's throwing up!" a crew member shouted. The door slammed behind them.

Jake turned to see his father staring at him.

"Jake?" Emory called. "Come over here. I just had an idea. Turn around."

"Huh? Turn around?" Jake obediently spun around.

"Yes!" Emory declared. "You have the same hair as Devon. You look almost like him — from behind."

"Wow. Thanks for the compliment," Jake joked, rolling his eyes.

A few of the extras laughed.

"This is an easy scene. Nothing to it," Emory

said, wrapping his arm heavily around Jake's shoulders.

"I — I don't understand," Jake stammered.

"We'll do the scene with you," Emory explained. "Get in the closet. And push at the door. Try to get out. That's all you have to do."

Jake stared at him in surprise. "Huh? Me? Do Devon's scene?"

"It's real easy, Jake," Emory replied, guiding him to the closet. "We shoot you from behind. No one will see your face. Come on. Let's get going."

Jake hesitated at the closet door. "You're sure?"

"You're not scared — are you, Jake?" Emory demanded.

"Scared? Of course not!" Jake declared. "Of course I'm not scared!"

He pulled open the closet door and stepped inside.

This is my chance, Jake decided.

My chance to prove to my dad that I'm not scared of anything.

"Quiet!" Sheila was shouting. "Quiet on the set! This is a take!"

ake wiped his sweaty hands off on his jeans legs. He cleared his throat and stepped up to the closet door.

Behind him, the camera operator whispered, "Not yet. I'll give you a signal."

"You okay in there, Jake?" Emory called. "Know what you have to do?"

"Just fine!" Jake called back. "I can handle it."

Yes, I can, he told himself. Yes, I can.

"We have a problem, Emory!" he heard Sheila shout.

"Problem? I'm about to start a take here," he heard Emory protest. "What's the problem?"

"Well . . . one of the snakes is missing."

From behind the closet door, Jake heard gasps and surprised cries from the extras in the classroom.

"One of the snakes got loose?" Emory asked.

"Yes. That's what the snake wrangler told me," Sheila replied. "It's got to be somewhere on the set. If you want to hold up the take and search for it —"

"What for?" Emory interrupted. "It's only one snake, right? And it's harmless?"

"Well . . . yes. But it's pretty big."

"We'll find it after we get the scene in the can," Emory declared. "I've wasted the whole morning. I can't stand to lose another minute."

Jake heard Emory muttering to someone for a few moments. Then he heard Sheila call, "Places. Get ready, everyone. Students, concentrate on your art projects."

"Quiet!"

"We're rolling," someone announced quietly. "We've got speed."

Jake's muscles tensed. He pressed both hands against the back of the door and took a deep breath.

"Scene one-twelve, take one," Jake heard Sheila announce. He heard the slap of a clapper.

"Wait for my signal," the camera operator repeated, whispering behind him. "And don't turn around. Just bang on the door, try the knob — then force the door open with your shoulder."

"No problem," Jake whispered back.

He took another deep breath and waited.

"Action!" he heard Emory call.

He heard voices in the classroom. Two girls were saying their lines.

He wondered how Chelsea was doing. She has the easy job, he thought.

What a weird day. When we came here this morning, I had no idea that the back of my head would become a *star*!

"Okay — go! Step up to the door — now." The camera operator's words broke into Jake's thoughts.

He took a step toward the door. Then another.

And as he took the final step, he felt the snake curl around his ankle.

10

A scream rose up from Jake's chest.

He shut his mouth tight to muffle it.

He knew the camera was running. He raised his fist to pound on the closet door.

But the snake tightened around his leg.

Tightened . . .

Until Jake had to scream. He couldn't hold it in any longer.

"Helllllp!" The shrill cry burst from Jake's mouth as he shoved open the door and staggered out into the classroom.

The snake tightened around his ankle. Refused to let go.

"Help me!" Jake gasped. "S-s-snake!"

He heard the startled cries of the other kids.

He saw his father's disgusted look.

Emory tossed his clipboard furiously to the floor. "Jake — what is your problem?" he demanded, storming across the floor, fists swinging at his sides.

"S-snake..." Jake mumbled, shaking his leg, hopping, jumping, trying to kick the creature off.

He lowered his gaze.

Not a snake.

No. No snake.

"Jake — your leg is tangled in a power cable," Emory sighed, hands on his waist. He rolled his eyes. His eyebrows rose about two feet on his forehead. "A power cable," he repeated disgustedly.

Jake bent down and pulled the cable off his ankle. He could hear the kids and crew members laughing at him.

When he stood up, Emory led him off the set. "If only you could admit that my movie sets frighten you," he said softly, "then I wouldn't force you to come to them."

"Emory, I wasn't scared. I —" Jake started.

But Devon Klar came jogging up to them. "Sorry about that," he told Emory. "I feel much better. I'm ready to do the scene."

"Good news," Emory replied. He patted Jake on the shoulder. "Why don't you go over there. Make yourself a sandwich. And wait till we're through with the scene."

"Yeah. Sure," Jake replied glumly.

Should I change my name to Loser? Or Wimp? Yeah. Wimp. That has a nice ring to it.

He trudged miserably to the food tables against the wall.

This is so crazy, he told himself.

I'm brave.

I love horror.

I love it as much as my dad.

I'm a scary guy too. I really am.

But how will I ever prove it to Emory? How?

Jake didn't feel much like eating. In fact, his stomach felt tied in knots and heavy as a rock.

But he picked up a plate and started to look over the sandwiches.

He took a ham sandwich and was spooning some potato salad onto his plate when he felt the snake slither between his legs.

After the snake incident, Emory didn't invite Jake back to the set. For the next few weeks, Jake and Chelsea hung out with Carlos, playing basketball and swimming in Jake's backyard.

One day they prowled around Hollywood Boulevard, checking out the T-shirt stores and the wax museum, like tourists. Another day, Jake's mom dropped them off in Westwood and they went shopping in the trendy little stores.

Jake was having an okay summer. But he couldn't stop thinking about his dad — about proving to Emory that he wasn't a wimp.

Jake went to the bookstore and bought a collection of Edgar Allan Poe stories. He sat out by the pool, hoping Emory would see him reading them.

Jake bought a bunch of magazines about horror

movies and left them around the house. He knew that might impress his dad.

But Emory was hard at work on his *Scream School* movie. He was seldom home. He didn't notice Jake's attempt to be a scary guy.

On the morning of his birthday, Jake pulled on a white polo shirt and faded jeans and hurried downstairs for breakfast. He expected his mom to make his favorite breakfast — blueberry pancakes with whipped cream.

But the maid told him she had already left the house. Jake found a note from his dad stuck on the refrigerator door:

> Happy Birthday, Jake!
> Wrapping up at the studio today. I'd like you to meet me there. I'll send a car for you.
> Mom will meet us at the studio, and we'll go out for a birthday dinner. Restaurant is your choice. But please don't say In & Out Burger. Let's pick something a little more festive.
> See you later. Love, Emory

The black limo pulled up the driveway at four o'clock. Since it was a birthday dinner, Jake had changed into clean khakis and a tan linen sports shirt that he usually wore only under protest.

The black-uniformed driver gave Jake a two-fingered salute. He had a bushy mustache and curly hair.

He held open the door for Jake and murmured, "Happy Birthday," as Jake climbed inside. Jake settled into the soft leather seat and gazed out through the tinted windows as the limo carried him silently to the movie studio.

The driver pulled the car past the guard booth at the front of the studio lot and stopped. The passenger door opened. Jake stared out at a little man who was holding the door for him.

"Welcome," the man said in a scratchy, hoarse voice.

Jake stepped out beside the little man. He was only a few inches taller than Jake.

He looked very old. He was entirely bald except for a few wisps of scraggly white hair that flew up around his ears. He had tiny, round gray eyes that squinted at Jake, half-opened and ringed by deep, dark circles.

His face was thin and powdery pale. His chin appeared to sag into the open collar of his white shirt.

The front of his shirt hung out over his suit pants. His shiny black suit was much too big. The jacket sleeves came down over his hands. The pants cuffs dragged on the pavement.

"This way," the little man croaked. He turned and began walking, his shoulders hunched, his eyes squinting ahead of him as if peering into a thick fog.

Who *is* this guy? Jake wondered. I've never seen him here before.

Jake followed him past the long white stucco building that housed the studio offices. They turned a corner and walked past the studio cafeteria, closed and dark.

Jake crossed a familiar walkway and started toward the soundstage, as big as an airplane hangar, where Emory had been filming.

But the little man grabbed Jake's sleeve. "This way," he said, pointing a bent, bony finger in the other direction.

The man's tiny gray eyes squinted hard at Jake.

He's so pale, Jake thought. How is it possible to live in sunny L.A. and be that pale?

He followed the little man away from the soundstage. The sun floated low in a smoggy sky. Jake felt the back of his neck prickle in the heat.

Where are we walking?

His pale head bobbing with each step, the man led Jake past another soundstage, past a city street set, past a Wild West town, past some low concrete buildings Jake didn't recognize.

Jake realized they were nearly at the back of the lot.

"You're taking me to my dad, right?" he asked.

The little man didn't reply. Instead, he pointed the same bony finger.

Jake saw a large green building up ahead. It looked as if it hadn't been used in a long while.

The green paint was peeling off the walls. The windows were all boarded up. A metal gutter had broken off from under the roof and hung down to the pavement.

"We're going in here?" Jake demanded, mopping sweat off his forehead with the back of his hand. "My dad is meeting me here?"

Again, the man didn't reply.

As Jake came closer, he could make out the faded words over the building's wooden door: SOUNDSTAGE 13.

Lucky thirteen, he thought.

Why is Emory using this old soundstage today? Must be for special effects or something.

"Is my mom here yet?" Jake asked. "She was supposed to meet us here."

The old man coughed in reply. He reached into the pocket of his baggy trousers and pulled out a set of keys. Big, metal, old-fashioned keys.

He fingered through the keys, squinting hard at them, holding them close to his face. He finally picked one and slid it into the lock on the door.

The door pushed open easily. The little man shoved it all the way, then stepped aside for Jake to enter.

"Hey — it's dark in here!" Jake protested. "Where are we?"

"Soundstage thirteen," the man replied from the doorway.

Jake took a deep breath, gazing into the darkness. The air felt hot and damp. It smelled stale in here. Sour.

"Is — is my dad working in here?" Jake demanded.

"I don't know anything about that," the little man replied.

"Huh? What do you mean?"

The man coughed again. The heavy keys jangled in his hand. "I had my instructions," he told Jake.

"Excuse me? Instructions?"

The door slammed shut.

Jake gasped. He stared into total darkness. "Hey, wait —"

Jake heard the key being turned in the lock.

"Hey, no!"

Jake leaped to the door. Fumbled in the dark for the knob.

Found it. Turned it. One way. The other way.

He pulled. Pulled with all his strength.

Locked. Locked in.

"Hey, let me out!" Jake cried. "What's the big idea? Let me out of here!"

12

Jake stepped back from the door.

The darkness seemed to close in on him.

He took a deep breath to calm himself — but almost choked on the sour smell.

What is this place? he wondered. He spun away from the door and waited for his eyes to adjust. Slender lines of sunlight filtered in between the boards over the windows.

The room was enormous. An old soundstage. Abandoned. Empty.

Jake cupped his hands around his mouth and called, "Emory? Emory? Are you here?"

His voice echoed off the walls and high ceiling.

No reply.

"Who was that freaky old guy?" Jake asked out loud. "And why did he bring me back here? Is it some kind of a joke?"

It didn't seem like a joke.

Jake's eyes slowly began to take in a few shapes, a few details. He saw a stack of wooden cartons against one wall. A rack of folding chairs all on their sides. Some metal trunks piled three high.

"It's a storage room," Jake muttered. "Why did the old guy lock me in a storage room?"

A square of pale orange light caught his eye. Far in the distance.

Another room?

Jake's shoes scraped over the concrete floor, kicking up clouds of dust as he made his way toward the light. "Hey — anybody there?" he called.

He listened to his echoing words.

"Hey — anybody?"

No answer.

He continued toward the light.

It's a way out, he thought. Yes! These sound-stages have doors at the side. And doors at the back. Doors all around.

This has got to lead to a way out.

His heart started to pound as he jogged across the enormous soundstage. Into the square of light.

Another room. The fading afternoon sunlight washing through a high window, a mile over Jake's head.

Jake stopped in the doorway and gazed into the room.

Costumes. Old-fashioned dresses and men's suits.

Rack after rack of old clothing. The costume racks, jammed so close together, filled the room.

Jake stared at cowboy outfits, ballet tutus, lace-covered ball gowns. . . .

He stepped into the room. Reached for the sleeve of an old army uniform. Covered in dust, he saw. Moths had shredded the cuff with a million tiny holes.

Jake moved between costume racks, studying the old dresses and uniforms and suits. His shoes slid on a thick layer of white powdery dust on the floor. The costumes were faded. Moth-eaten. Dusty.

No one has been in here for a hundred years! Jake thought. Weird!

He made his way to the center of the room. And stopped at a pile of old costumes, thrown in a heap on the floor.

A furry gorilla costume lay tangled in a silky black cape. Jake bent down and pulled the gorilla costume free. It weighed a ton. And smelled like spoiled meat.

Jake held it up, studying the faded rubber gorilla face. "Cool," he murmured.

He dropped the costume back onto the pile.

And as he dropped it, he saw the pile move.

The black cape appeared to shiver. Two long blue ball gowns ruffled, then slid apart.

"Huh?" Jake gasped as the costumes shifted. Sleeves shot up as if reaching for something. Dresses rolled over. A brown army uniform tumbled off the pile.

And as Jake stared in amazement, two figures rose slowly from the middle of the pile.

Two ugly, pale-faced figures, stretching their arms, rolling their heads on their necks, climbing up, floating up from under the dusty pile of costumes.

"No way —" Jake blurted out. He took a step back and bumped into a rack of fur coats.

The two figures continued to stretch. One was a man, the other a woman. Their faces were ghoulish. Skin pulled so tight Jake could see the bone underneath. Eyes yellow, sunken back in their sockets. Their lips cracked and purple.

"Let's make a movie, Jake," the woman croaked. Her voice as dry as the crackle of dead leaves. She stepped out from the pile of costumes, her sunken eyes locked on Jake, her purple lips twisted in an ugly smile.

"Huh?" Jake backed into the fur coats. Tried to slide away. But he was trapped between the costume racks.

"Wh-who are you?" he choked out. "How do you know my name?"

The man lurched forward beside the woman. He licked his lips with a fat purple tongue. He had a deep red scar up and down one side of his face. The scar ran all the way up through his patchy brown hair. Dried blood was caked all along the scar.

The two ghoulish figures were both dressed in black. Loose-fitting black robes that slid silently along the floor as they stepped away from the costume pile.

And moved toward Jake.

"Leave me alone!" Jake screamed angrily. "What's going on here, anyway?"

"Let's make our own horror movie," the woman rasped.

"But who are you?" Jake demanded. "What are you doing here?"

"We were abandoned, Jake," the man replied, his voice a dry whisper like his partner's.

"This is a forgotten set," the woman croaked. "They forgot about us back here. Forgot all about us."

"But we're still here," the man added, licking his cracked lips again, his sunken yellow eyes rolling wildly in their sockets. "We're still here — and now we've got you."

"But — but —" Jake sputtered.

"Now we can make our movie," the woman said, floating closer, arms outstretched, side by side with the man. "Now we can make the most horrifying movie ever made!"

Jake was trapped. He couldn't run. Couldn't move.

The two ghouls grabbed him by the shoulders. Lifted him off the floor. Shoved him back against the costume rack.

"Show time," they whispered.

13

"Let go of me!" Jake shrieked. "Put me down!"

The two ghouls held him off the floor. Their purple mouths spread in gleeful grins.

"Don't you want to make a movie with us, Jake?" the woman rasped.

"Don't you want to be our star?" her partner whispered.

"No! Put me down!" Jake insisted angrily. "Take me to my father — right now!"

"But we don't know your father," the man replied.

"We've been locked in here for so many years," the woman said, shaking her head. Her dry, strawlike hair brushed Jake's cheek. "We've been waiting here for so long . . . waiting for our *star*!"

"You're crazy!" Jake cried. "You're both crazy! Let go of me!"

"We're going to have some fun," the man said, lowering Jake to the floor. "Our movie is going to be the most terrifying ever made."

"You'll both be terrified when my dad finds out you're here!" Jake threatened.

They both tossed back their heads and laughed.

"Your dad can't do anything to us," the woman said.

"Because we're dead," her partner added. "What can you do to someone who's already dead?" He ran his fingers down the caked blood along his deep scar.

They both laughed again, dry, hoarse laughter that sounded more like coughing.

I've got to get out of here, Jake thought.

They're both totally nuts! I've got to find a way out.

He began inching along the costume rack, his eyes searching the room for a door or window.

He stopped when the costume pile in the center of the floor began to move again.

Coats and dresses shook. The gorilla costume rolled over.

Two more ugly figures climbed up from beneath the pile. Two men. With long, dry hair like white straw, greenish skin, and frightening, purple-lipped grins.

They stood up, stretching, groaning as if they hadn't moved in a hundred years.

"Noooo," a low moan escaped Jake's throat.

"Our cast is here!" the woman cried, moving to Jake's side. Her fingers dug into the shoulder of his shirt.

"We can begin our movie!" the man declared. "We are here. At last, we are all here!"

Jake pulled free of the woman's sharp grasp. He was breathing hard. His heart thudded against his chest.

"This is a joke — right?" he choked out. "This is some kind of a joke?"

One of the scraggly haired, yellow-eyed men vanished into the racks of costumes. A few seconds later, he returned, carrying a long stick in front of him like a flagpole.

Jake gasped.

What was that perched on top of the stick?

A head?

A human head?

Jake squinted up at it — and then opened his mouth in a shrill cry of horror when he recognized it.

Chelsea.

Chelsea's head.

ake shut his eyes and staggered back.

His stomach lurched as he fell against a rack of costumes. His throat tightened. He couldn't breathe.

He toppled back into the costumes. And fell through to the other side.

Dazed, dizzy, he scrambled to his knees. And half-ran, half-crawled through the next costume rack.

He burst through the other side. And saw an open door at the far wall.

Yes!

Struggling to breathe, his chest pounding, his ears ringing, he forced himself to his feet. And took off.

He didn't turn back. But he could hear the rapid footsteps of the four ghouls close behind him.

"Come back, Jake!"

"Don't you want to be a *star*?"

"We need you, Jake! We need your *head*!"

"Nooooo!" a terrified howl escaped Jake's throat. He was running now, running full speed.

Through the doorway. Into a long, narrow hall.

"You can be a star with your friend, Jake!"

"Your friend is waiting here for you!"

"Give us your head! We need your head!"

Jake's shoes slid as he followed the hallway around a sharp turn. He could hear the four ghouls behind him, close, so close. They called to him in their hoarse, raspy voices, begging him to stop, to come back, to surrender his head . . .

. . . like Chelsea.

He didn't realize he had started to sob. Hot tears ran down his cheeks, flew off his face as he tore down the long hall.

He made another sharp turn — and ran into a pile of metal equipment. Old cameras. Sound amps.

They blocked the hall.

Nowhere to run.

Strong arms tackled Jake from behind.

"Where were you going, Jake?"

"You can't leave. We need our star!"

"Noooo!" With an angry cry of protest, Jake swung his elbows hard. Pushed back the ghoulish attacker.

Clawed his way frantically over the old, dusty equipment.

A hand grabbed his ankle.

Jake kicked himself free.

"Come back, Jake!"

"You can't escape us!"

"Give us your head!"

Sobbing, his chest heaving, his side aching, Jake scrambled across the floor.

And fell facedown in front of a dark curtain.

Bony hands grabbed his ankles.

Can't move, he realized.

They've got me. I can't move another step.

He couldn't hold back the tears. His whole body shook in terror.

He hunched on his knees on the floor and waited. Waited for the ghouls to drag him away.

He heard a creaking sound.

And saw the curtain in front of him sway.

And then rise.

The curtain pulled up rapidly.

And Jake, on his knees, sobbing loudly, stared out at a roomful of people. Balloons. Party hats.

Dozens of grinning faces.

"Surprise!"

"Happy Birthday!"

surprise party, Jake realized to his horror.

He saw his mom and dad in the front. Carlos stood with Chelsea.

Chelsea?

The head was a fake.

Everything was a fake.

All a joke. All a stupid joke.

And here he was, on his knees in front of everyone he knew, crying his eyes out, shaking like a baby.

The cheers and happy cries died instantly. Troubled, confused whispers filled the big room.

"Jake — what's wrong?" Chelsea cried.

The actors who played the ghouls hurried to help Jake to his feet. "Sorry," one of them whispered. "Did we go a little too far?"

"We thought you were in on it," another one said. "Your father told us to give you a good scare."

Jake turned to find his mom and dad beside him. Mrs. Banyon wrapped Jake in a hug and turned angrily to Emory. "I *told* you it was a stupid idea. You *ruined* his birthday!"

"But — but —" Emory sputtered. "He always tells me he isn't scared. He always tells me he's as brave as I am. So I decided to believe him. I thought he'd *enjoy* it!"

Jake's mom shook her head angrily. "You won't give up — will you, Emory? You have to prove to your own son that you're the King of Horror."

She hugged Jake tighter. He had stopped sobbing, but he couldn't stop the trembling.

"Mom, please —" he whispered. "Let go. Everyone is watching."

She ignored him and kept her angry glare on Emory. "Just apologize to Jake. Go ahead. Apologize."

"Mom — please!" Jake begged.

Total silence had fallen over the room. Jake could see all his friends, his relatives, his parents' friends — all watching him.

I've never been so embarrassed in my life, he thought.

How could Emory do this to me?

How could he hire these actors to *terrify* me on my birthday?

And now I'll *never* be able to prove to him that I'm not scared of his movies.

Never.

Emory leaned close to Jake and began to apologize. "I'm really sorry if I —"

Jake didn't wait to hear any more.

The staring people . . . the silence in the room . . . the embarrassment . . . the embarrassment.

Enough! he thought.

He broke free of his mother's hug — and ran.

He ran through the open curtain. Back into the long hall.

He didn't know where he was running. He just wanted to run forever.

Emory will never let me forget this, he thought bitterly. Emory will never let me live this down.

But — a few weeks later — Emory had a *big* surprise for him that would change everything.

•

hot July afternoon, the sun blazing down. Jake and Emory were in the swimming pool. Jake floated lazily on a blue vinyl raft. Emory splashed noisily past him, bobbing up, then beneath the surface like a hairy porpoise, doing his usual one hundred laps.

"One hundred!" he cried, surfacing finally at the shallow end. Water ran off him as he stood. He pulled off his goggles and tossed them onto the deck.

Emory swept back his thick mop of black hair. Water clung to his bushy eyebrows. "Jake, are you getting too much sun?" he asked.

"I put on lotion," Jake replied, paddling the raft lazily with both hands. "Number fifteen, I think."

Emory grabbed the end of the raft and pulled it into the shallow end. "I want to talk to you," he said.

Jake squinted up at him through his sunglasses. "Did I do something wrong?"

Emory smiled. "No. I have some news." He ducked under the water. Came up quickly and spit a stream of water onto Jake's chest.

Jake laughed. "Hey — is that your news?"

"No," Emory laughed. "I just wanted to get your attention."

His expression turned serious. "The studio wants me to start *Scream School VI* right away. We're going to film on location. I found this old, abandoned high school out in the desert. It's perfect-looking, and it's supposed to be haunted."

"Cool," Jake interrupted. "Maybe you can film real ghosts!"

"I'd rather film actors," Emory replied, smiling. "They're a little easier to control."

He wiped water from his eyebrows, then slapped a fly that had perched on his shoulder. "Anyway, Jake, I want you to come on location with me."

Jake nearly toppled off the raft. "Excuse me?"

"Your mom has to visit her sister for a week. I don't want you staying home by yourself with the housekeeper," Emory replied.

He swirled the raft around. "We'll have fun," he told Jake. "And I promise I won't do anything to scare you."

"I don't get scared on your movie sets," Jake insisted quietly.

"Whatever," Emory said, ducking his broad shoulders under the water. "Anyway, you can help out on the set — but only if you want to."

Jake squinted up at his dad. "It's a haunted old school, abandoned in the desert?"

Emory nodded. "What do you think? Want to come?"

"Sounds great!" Jake exclaimed. "I'm there!"

This is my chance, he thought, gazing up at Emory's pleased smile.

This is my chance to show him how brave I am.

Jake didn't realize how right he was.

"We need to break some of the windows," Emory instructed a crew member. "And can we spray a layer of dust over the wood down here? And get some more dust over the windows?"

The young man hurried to carry out Emory's orders. Other movie workers were setting up cameras and sound equipment at the front of the school.

Jake gazed up at the abandoned high school. It was three stories tall, built of redwood logs that had faded and peeled under the hot desert sun. The clock in a small tower on the slanting slate roof had no hands. The flagpole tilted against the side of the building.

Shielding his eyes from the glare of sunlight, Jake gazed down the street. A row of low stucco houses had also been abandoned. Across from them, a tilting wooden sign in front of a rail fence proclaimed: 3B RANCH. HORSES.

Jake didn't see any horses behind the fence. And he didn't see any ranchers.

He and Emory had arrived in Silver City two days before. They were staying in their air-conditioned movie trailer. The little hotel in town was closed and boarded up.

In two days, Jake had seen only five or six people in the town.

Why do people build a town and then abandon it? he wondered.

In the far distance, Jake could see brown and purple mountains poking up through a yellow haze. The Sierra Nevadas, he knew.

He had studied a map on the drive across the desert. Silver City was a tiny dot near the Nevada border.

"Whoa. Watch it."

Jake stepped out of the way as two men hurried past, setting down electrical cables. He wandered over to the food table in the shade of a trailer.

The actor who played Johnny Scream sat in the open trailer doorway, moving his lips silently as he read through a pink copy of the script. His name was Rad Donner. Without the gruesome makeup, he was handsome and young-looking, with straight blond hair cut very short, freckles on his cheeks, and a warm smile.

He flashed his warm smile at Jake. "Hey. What's up?"

"Just watching everyone," Jake mumbled. He picked up a slice of watermelon from the table. "Wow. It's hot in the sun!"

"The desert," Rad replied, eyes on his script. "It's even hotter inside the school. You been in there?"

"Not yet." Jake took a big bite of watermelon.

"Your dad knows how to pick creepy locations," Rad said, grinning. "Hey — did he tell you about the *Johnny Scream* CD-ROM game?"

Jake shook his head. "No."

"It made number one best-selling game. Cool, huh? Have you played it?"

"Emory brought it home, but I haven't opened it yet."

"Well, I have my laptop in my trailer, if you want to check it out later," Rad offered. "You know. If you get bored or something."

Jake started to thank him but heard Emory calling. He turned and hurried across the sand and tall grass to see what his father wanted.

"We're shooting exteriors today," Emory said, scribbling something on his clipboard. "Just some outside shots of the school. But tomorrow I hope to shoot in the lunchroom."

A cloud rolled over the sun, sending a blue shadow sweeping across the ground and then the school. Emory mopped his forehead and adjusted the *Johnny Scream* baseball cap over his eyes.

"Want to go inside and scout out the lunchroom for me?" he asked Jake.

"Yeah. Sure," Jake answered quickly.

"If you're scared, you can say no."

Jake frowned at his dad. "No problem!"

"See how much work has to be done in there," Emory instructed. "I think it's in back on the first floor. Or else it's in the basement."

"I'll find it," Jake told him. He turned and jogged toward the school.

Near the entrance, two crew members held long-nozzled machines like paint sprayers. They were spraying a layer of dust on the front wall.

Jake climbed the broken stairs and pulled open the front door. A blast of hot, musty air greeted him. He stepped into the front hall and waited for his eyes to adjust to the dim light.

A glass trophy case against the wall stood open. One silver trophy lay on its side. The other shelves were empty.

Draped over the front hall, a torn and faded blue banner read: GO, PIRATES!

Jake's shoes thudded loudly on the hard floor as he passed a door marked FRONT OFFICE and began making his way down the hall. Lockers stood open. Empty. One row of lockers had been pulled in the diary? Did he follow the directions and mix it himself?

And drink it?

Was my uncle the beast that was terrifying Shepherd Falls?

I couldn't stay here if he was.

I was in terrible danger.

I had to learn the truth — fast.

But how?

Lying in bed, tossing from side to side, wide awake, I thought of a plan.

I waited until after dinner the next night. Then I hid in Uncle Jekyll's lab.

18

found the lab door closed. I turned the knob, pulled the door open, and crept inside.

The equipment churned and bubbled. On the long lab table, I saw two glass beakers half-filled with a purple liquid. A clear liquid dripped from a glass tube into a gallon-sized bottle.

Uncle Jekyll and Marianna were still at the dinner table. We'd had a quiet — almost silent — dinner. Marianna kept casting angry glances at her father. Uncle Jekyll pretended to ignore them.

"Are you going out tonight?" he asked her.

An odd question. I'd never seen Marianna leave the house.

"I don't know what I'm doing," she mumbled into her tuna casserole.

I asked to be excused, saying I didn't want any dessert.

I knew I had very little time to hide. My uncle always headed straight for his lab after dinner.

My eyes searched the long, cluttered room. Where could I hide? Where could I hide safely but still be able to spy on Uncle Jekyll?

A row of dark metal supply closets across from the lab table caught my eye. They looked like the hall lockers at my old school.

I darted over to them and began pulling open the doors one at a time. The narrow closets were all jammed with equipment. No room for me.

I heard Uncle Jekyll's voice out in the hall. He was arguing again with Marianna.

I searched desperately for a hiding place.

I'm going to be caught! I realized. He'll ask me what I'm doing in here. And I won't have an answer.

My heart thudding in my chest, I pulled open the last closet door. Yes! Only a few towels on the bottom.

I took a deep breath and squeezed inside. I pulled the metal door nearly closed — just as Uncle Jekyll stepped into the lab.

Peering through the narrow opening, I held my breath. Did he see me swing the door shut? Could he hear my heart pounding like a bass drum?

He moved to the table and inspected the beakers with the purple liquid.

He didn't see me, I realized. I slumped against the back of the closet and slowly let my breath out.

He poured the purple liquid carefully into a rack of slender glass test tubes. Then he adjusted some dials on the electronic equipment at the end of the table.

What is he working on? I wondered.

He is working so fast, so urgently. He must be in his lab at least twenty hours a day.

Why is he working so hard? What is he trying to do?

I hope it is something *good*, I prayed. I hope his work has nothing to do with the creature that is wrecking the village.

Maybe he's trying to cure a disease, I told myself. Maybe he's very close. He has almost found the cure. And he is working day and night because he knows he almost has it.

Or maybe he is in a race with another doctor. Uncle Jekyll wants to cure the disease before the other doctor beats him to it.

I desperately wanted my uncle to be *good*. I didn't want him to be a mad scientist. An evil villain. A . . . creature.

Please . . . I prayed . . . Please don't drink your formula and turn into a growling beast. Please . . . let the people in the town be wrong about you.

I watched as his hands moved furiously over the table. Pouring clear liquids into purple liquids. Turning knobs and dials. Mixing chemicals from one test tube to another. Holding glass beakers over a flame until the liquid inside bubbled and steamed.

Electricity sizzled over the table. Uncle Jekyll kept shocking the dark liquid in a beaker with some sort of electric probe.

His head bent, his shoulders slumped under the white lab coat, he worked feverishly, without ever stopping for a second, without coming up for air.

I began to feel cramped in the narrow closet. My knees ached. My back ached. Pressed against the metal sides, my arms had fallen asleep.

This was a big mistake, I decided. I'm not going to see anything interesting at all. I should have trusted Uncle Jekyll. I shouldn't be hiding in here spying on him.

I watched him raise a test tube to the fluorescent light over the table. It contained a rust-colored liquid that glowed in the light.

He studied it for a moment, turning it between his fingers.

Then he tilted back his head. Lowered the test tube to his mouth.

And drank the liquid down.

Oh, no, I thought, feeling heavy dread knot my throat. I pressed a hand over my mouth to keep from crying out.

Uncle Jekyll licked his lips. Then he raised another test tube with a green liquid inside — and poured that down his throat too.

He swallowed noisily and licked his lips.

Then he braced himself. He flattened both hands on the tabletop and leaned forward. As if waiting for the liquids to do something to him.

I stared through the narrow opening. I couldn't breathe. I couldn't move.

Leaning hard against the tabletop, Uncle Jekyll shut his eyes. His mouth twisted. His knees started to collapse.

Grabbing the tabletop to keep himself standing, he opened his mouth in a shrill howl of pain.

His eyes bulged and rolled in his head.

His face turned bright red.

Another painful howl escaped his throat. An animal howl. A *wolf* howl.

He clamped his eyes shut. He pounded the table with both hands. He tore at his white hair until it stood up in wild tufts.

His whole face twisted in agony.

And then, with an ugly groan from deep in his belly, he spun away from the table. And staggered to the door. Staggered like an animal, moaning and growling.

And vanished from the lab.

My heart throbbed. My chest ached. I realized I'd been holding my breath the whole time. I let it out in a loud whoosh.

I pushed open the closet door with my shoulder. And half fell, half leaped out of the narrow closet.

"I don't *believe* it," I murmured. "He *is* the beast. Uncle Jekyll *is* the creature."

My head spun. I raised both hands to my cheeks. My skin was burning hot!

What can I do? I asked myself.

Who can I tell?

I've got to stop him. I've got to get help for him.

But who can help?

I couldn't think clearly. I couldn't think of anything at all.

I kept seeing the tortured expression on Uncle Jekyll's face. And hearing the animal howls that burst from his throat.

I stared at the empty test tubes lying on their sides on the table. How could he drink that stuff? *How?*

I've got to get out of here, I decided.

I turned to the door — and screamed.

Uncle Jekyll stood inside the doorway.

He had returned to the lab!

He was breathing hard, grunting with each breath, staring at me. Staring angrily.

"Heidi," he growled. "I'm so sorry you saw."

e lumbered toward me, his eyes rolling wildly.

"Wh-what are you going to do?" I stammered. I backed away from him, backed up until I hit the metal closets.

He grunted in reply. And grabbed my arm with both hands.

"Uncle Jekyll — stop!" I cried. "What are you doing?"

"Sorry you saw," he rasped again. His chest heaved up and down. His breath came in hoarse wheezes.

"Let go!" I pleaded.

But his grip tightened, and he pulled me away from the closets. I tried to pull back, but he was too strong.

He dragged me from the lab. Up the stairs. And pushed me into my room.

I spun around to face him. "Why are you doing this?" I cried.

He lurched into the hall and slammed the bedroom door shut. I heard the lock click.

I dove to the door. "Uncle Jekyll — I can help you! Let me help you! Don't lock me in here. Why are you doing this?"

"For your own good," he replied in a hoarse animal growl.

I heard his heavy footsteps going down the stairs.

I tried the door. Locked. He locked me in.

"Uncle Jekyll —" I called.

I knew he couldn't hear me. I heard the front door slam.

I ran to the bedroom window and peered out into the darkness.

After a few seconds, he staggered into view. I took a deep breath and tried to slow my racing heart as I watched him make his way down the hill toward the village. After a minute or so, he disappeared into the shadows.

"Why?" I murmured, shaking my head. "Why?"

Does he plan to keep me locked up in here forever? I asked myself.

No. He can't.

And then I thought of an even more frightening

question: What does he plan to do with me when he gets back?

Through the open window, I heard a shrill scream. And then frightened shouts from down the hill.

"I have to get out of here," I told myself.

I tried tugging the doorknob with all my strength. Then I tried to batter the door open with my shoulder.

No way. The door was solid oak.

I dove to the window. I heard more screams from town. Flames shot up. More angry cries. A siren wailed.

I leaned out the window and looked down. A two-story drop straight to the ground. No tree to climb down. No shrubs below to break my fall.

"I can't jump out," I decided. "I'll break my neck."

Then I spotted the metal rain gutter at the corner of the house. Rusted, its paint peeling, it ran along the roof, then straight down nearly to the ground.

If I can wrap my hands around it, I can slide down, I decided. But will it hold my weight?

Only one way to find out.

I leaned farther out the window and reached for it . . . reached . . .

No. It was inches from my grasp. I couldn't lean any farther. I couldn't reach it.

Wait, I thought. I ducked back into the room and pulled the desk chair to the window. My legs trembling, I climbed onto the desk chair. Then I leaned out the window again.

Reached . . . reached for the gutter.

My fingers brushed the rusted metal —

— and then I lost my balance.

I felt my body plunging forward . . . plunging out the window . . .

. . . and I fell.

20

I screamed — and grabbed wildly for the gutter.

My hands wrapped around it. The rusted metal scraped my skin.

I cried out and held on. Sliding . . . sliding too fast.

The pain grew too intense.

My hands flew off the gutter.

I landed hard on my back.

I didn't feel the landing. I didn't feel anything.

My wind was knocked out. I gasped for breath.

I'm dying, I thought.

But then I pulled in a wheezing breath. And, ignoring the pain, forced it out.

Above me, the house came back into view. And above it, the sky, pink with a high blanket of gray clouds.

I sucked in another breath. Another. The air felt so cool.

I began to feel again. Felt the snow on the back of my neck. Felt the cold dampness of the ground through my clothes.

My hands throbbed and burned, burned from sliding on the rusted metal gutter.

I sat up.

And heard a scream. And sirens down the hill.

"Uncle Jekyll —" I choked out.

I climbed unsteadily to my feet. The ground rocked and bobbed beneath me. I shut my eyes, waiting for my legs to stop trembling.

"I'm okay," I murmured. I bent down and rubbed cold snow on my burning hands.

Then I began jogging down the hill.

What did I plan to do when I reached the village?

I didn't know. I couldn't think clearly. But I had nowhere else to run.

Maybe I can save Uncle Jekyll, I thought.

A deafening explosion made me stop. Somewhere in the village a mountain of flames burst up like a volcano erupting.

Shrill screams and cries rose up over the roar of the flames. In the flickering yellow-orange light, I could see people running frantically in all directions.

Maybe I can pull Uncle Jekyll away from there, I thought.

I instantly realized it was a crazy idea.

He was a *beast* now, an inhuman creature.

He had to be stopped.

Breathing hard, I reached the edge of the village. I heard the crack of gunshots. I ran past an overturned car, its tires spinning.

I turned onto the main street. Police officers patrolled, guns out, ready for action. In the orange light of the fires, their faces were grim and angry.

"Get away from here!" a man shouted.

It took me a few seconds to realize he was shouting at me.

"Stay out of town!"

"The beast is angry tonight!"

"Get off the street!"

Their shouts rang out over the crackling of the fires, the wail of sirens, the terrified screams. They hurried away, toward a burning house on the next block.

I turned, eager to get off the street.

Too late.

"Noooooo!" I uttered a shocked scream as the creature leaped out from the side of a house.

A wolf! A snarling wolf-creature, howling, snapping his wet jaws. His gray-and-brown fur bristling. Lumbering forward stiffly on two legs.

His red eyes glowed and then locked on me.

I backed across a snow-covered lawn. Too late to run.

Too late to hide.

The growling creature moved quickly, arching his body for the attack.

I searched frantically for a weapon. A stick. A tree branch. Something to use to bat it away.

No. Nothing.

With a hideous roar, the beast spread his furry arms — and dove at me.

21

With a terrified cry, I dropped to the ground. My face plunged into the hard-packed snow.

I jerked my head up in time to see the beast sail over me.

I tried to scramble away.

But before I could climb to my feet, I felt a heavy paw on my back.

"No!" I gasped.

Grunting loudly, the beast pushed me down. Held me down on the snow.

"Uncle Jekyll —" I choked out. "Please . . ."

I turned and saw him tilt up his head and send an animal roar to the sky.

And then I saw a figure come running across the street.

Aaron!

21

ake sat across from Emory in their trailer. They both sipped from cans of Coke.

The air conditioner rattled and shook. But it felt good to escape the blazing-hot desert air.

"Emory — you promised you wouldn't do anything to scare me," Jake said, brushing his dark hair off his forehead with his free hand.

"I know. I know," Emory muttered. "I didn't have anything to do with that scene in the lunchroom. I'm not trying to scare you, Jake."

Emory raised his right hand. "I swear."

"Then who messed up the food?" Jake demanded. He took a long, cold sip of soda.

"That's what I'm trying to find out!" Emory declared. "Probably some joker who —"

"I was talking to one of the extras," Jake interrupted. "And she told me the school is really haunted. She said it was built on a graveyard, and —"

"I heard that story," Emory muttered again. "It's just silly. You don't believe it — do you?"

Jake shrugged. "I don't know. I —"

Emory's cell phone rang. He clicked it open. "Yeah? Yeah? No one in the food crew? You asked them all? Did you talk to the caterer?"

He lowered the phone and talked to Jake. "No one knows anything about the lunchroom food. It's a total mystery."

Emory returned to the phone. "Okay. Okay. I'm coming. We've *got* to accomplish *something* today!"

He clicked the phone shut, stuffed it in his pocket, and jumped to his feet. "We're going to try the cheerleader scene behind the school while the sun is still up. Come on. This should be an easy one."

Five of the extras had been chosen to be cheerleaders. Jake saw Mindy adjusting the short red-and-white skirt of her uniform as he followed his father behind the school.

She smiled at him as he came near. "Isn't this exciting?" she gushed. "I get to be in the cheerleader scene."

"That's awesome!" Jake agreed.

Emory hurried to check with Sheila and other

members of the crew. Guys scurried around, carrying cables, moving lights. A young woman was concentrating on snapping a new lens onto the camera.

"Are you okay?" Jake asked Mindy. "I mean, after the lunchroom."

She shrugged. "I guess. That was totally gross."

"Emory can't figure out how it happened," Jake said.

Mindy's green eyes flashed. "Bet I can tell him how it happened!"

"Where are you putting the girls?" Emory was asking a crew member in white shorts and a white short-sleeved sports shirt. "Over there?"

The man pointed to a large square of dirt beyond the tall grass. "They'll have the sun behind them. It'll look great, Emory."

Emory squinted at the area, then nodded. "Okay. Are we ready for a run-through?"

"When are we reshooting the lunchroom scene?" Sheila asked Emory.

Emory frowned. "As soon as we can get a new shipment of food." He rolled his eyes. "Maybe the next batch won't have human body parts in it."

Sheila shook her head. "They weren't real, were they?"

"No," Emory replied bitterly. "But they *looked* real enough. The kids believed it."

Sheila hurried over to the five girls in cheerleader uniforms. "Ready, girls? Do you know your routine?"

"We've been practicing for an hour," Mindy told her.

"Well, let's see what you can do." Sheila turned to Emory. "They're ready to start. Want to watch?"

"Yes. Let's do it," Emory replied. He tugged his baseball cap down lower on his forehead. Then he put an arm on Jake's shoulder and led him to the filming area.

"Everyone, let's hear your cheer," Sheila instructed. "Nice and loud, okay?"

Mindy and the other four girls lined up on the edge of the tall grass. Behind them, purple mountains rose in the hazy distance. A red hawk circled low in the sunlit sky.

They began their cheer:

"GO PIRATES

GO PIRATES

LISTEN TO US SCREAM!

GO PIRATES

GO PIRATES

WE'LL SCREAM A LITTLE LOUDER!"

They repeated the cheer, louder this time. Then a third time, even louder.

"That's excellent," Emory told them, clapping his hands. "We want it loud and shrill." He turned to the camera operator. "Everything set?"

Squinting into the viewer, the man nodded. "Looking good, Emory."

"Get them in position," Emory instructed Sheila.

Sheila guided the five cheerleaders over the grass. "Onto that dirt area," she told them. "We'll do a run-through of the whole routine first."

Mindy led the way off the grass, onto the dirt. The five girls were chatting excitedly.

The chatting stopped as Mindy cried out.

Jake saw her arms fly straight up. Then she went sliding onto her back.

"Oh — oww!" Mindy cried. She kicked her legs up. "It's muddy! It's all *muddy*!"

Mindy reached a hand up to another girl. The girl started to help Mindy up — slipped — and they both tumbled into the mud.

"Whoa!" Another cheerleader slid. Caught her balance. Then fell facedown with a wet splash.

She pulled herself up slowly, covered with thick mud from head to foot.

"What's *happening*?" Emory cried, dropping his clipboard.

"It's all muddy!" Mindy shrieked. "Our uniforms — my *hair*! Oh, no — *my hair*! Yuck!"

"But how can it be muddy?" Emory demanded furiously. "It hasn't rained here in weeks!"

One of the girls tried to wipe the mud off her face, but only smeared it. The girl next to her pulled a thick, wet clump from her blond hair and tossed it with a *PLOP* to the ground.

"This can't be happening!" Emory screamed. "There can't be mud here in the desert! There can't!"

And then Mindy uttered a low groan. Her eyes bulged wide, and she dropped to her knees.

She pulled something from the mud.

Something smooth and gray.

She held it up in a trembling hand.

"A s-skull!" she stammered. "A human skull!"

22

he next morning, the camera lens was missing. Two of the main electrical cables had been cut in half. The trophy case in the school's front hall had been filled with tarantulas.

Shooting had to be stopped while repairs were made.

That afternoon, Jake found his dad behind their trailer. "I don't know what's going on," Emory said excitedly into his cell phone. "Maybe this old school really *is* haunted!"

He turned and saw Jake standing behind him. "Oh, hi." He clicked the phone shut. "Didn't see you there."

"Do you really think the school is haunted?" Jake asked softly.

"No. Of course not," Emory replied quickly.

But Jake caught a flicker of fear in his father's eyes.

"Well . . . if it's not ghosts . . ." Jake started.

"It's some wise guy on the set," Emory said, knitting his bushy eyebrows angrily. "Maybe someone on the crew who has a grudge of some kind."

Jake stared hard at his dad. "A crew guy? Is that *really* what you believe?"

"Stop looking at me like that!" Emory snapped. "I don't know *what* to believe. But I sure don't believe in *ghosts*!"

He tugged Jake's hand. "Come with me. Let's check some things out."

He led Jake past busy crew members, past a group of extras finishing their lunches in the shade of the building. Into the school.

The trophy case had been cleaned out. The tarantulas taken out to the desert.

Carpenters hammered and sawed, getting a classroom ready for filming.

His head bobbing with each step, his expression unhappy, Emory led Jake down the long hall. They turned a corner and climbed the dust-covered stairs to the second floor.

Down another long hall, walking quickly side by side.

Jake stopped when he heard a sound behind them.

Footsteps?

Emory heard it too. He glanced back.

No one there.

They walked another few steps. And heard the sound again.

A scrape. A soft thud.

They waited, listening.

Another scraping footstep. Closer now.

Jake turned and gazed behind them.

"No. No one there," he told Emory in a whisper.

Emory shrugged.

They walked a little farther down the dimly lit hall.

SCRAPE. THUD.

So close now. So close behind them.

They both spun around at the same time.

And gasped when they saw no one.

"This is kind of creepy," Jake confessed in a whisper.

"Stay calm," Emory replied, placing a hand on his shoulder. "Just keep walking. There isn't any-one there."

"But I *heard* —" Jake insisted.

"Just keep walking." Emory gave him a little push. "I think it's just some kind of echo."

They started walking again.

"Where are we going?" Jake asked.

Before Emory could answer, they heard laugh-ter.

Soft. Muffled, as if it were floating to them from far away.

Jake's voice caught in his throat. "Did you hear that?" he choked out.

Emory nodded, his eyes wide.

He's afraid, Jake thought. I think he's actually afraid.

They heard another burst of laughter, high, tinny laughter.

"Must be coming from outside," Emory murmured. "Must be those extra kids out there."

"But they were in the front of the building," Jake said. "We're in the back."

Emory scratched his chin. They turned a corner and started down another long hall. "There's no one else in the building," Emory murmured. "The laughter has to be from outside. You know. Sound carries strangely in these old buildings."

Jake swallowed. "Right."

They began walking faster, as if trying to get away from whatever was following them.

"I'm looking for the wood shop," Emory said. "I thought we might do a very scary scene —"

He stopped as another wave of laughter burst through the hallway, echoing off the tile walls.

Jake heard voices. Kids talking. More laughter.

He pointed. "It — it's coming from that classroom!" he exclaimed.

He saw Emory hesitate.

He's frightened, Jake realized. But he can't let on. For my sake.

Another burst of laughter.

Jake followed his dad to the classroom door. He could hear the voices inside the room.

Emory took a deep breath — and pushed open the door.

They both peered inside.

Dark in the room. Empty. Overturned desks. A wastebasket standing upside down on the teacher's desk.

No one in there. No one.

"But I heard them," Emory murmured.

They both gasped when they heard more high, shrill laughter. From the next room.

Jake and Emory raced toward the sound. Emory got there first. He shoved open the door.

Silence now.

No one in there.

"I don't *believe* this!" Emory cried, sweat glistening on his forehead and on his black eyebrows. "What's going on? *Who* is doing this?"

Jake grabbed his dad's shirt sleeve. "Emory — you promised me."

Emory turned, his face tight with confusion. "Huh?"

"You promised me," Jake repeated. "You said you wouldn't test me anymore. You said you wouldn't do anything frightening."

"But — but —" Emory sputtered. "But I'm not doing it!"

23

ohnny Scream stood leaning against a power saw in the wood shop. The tall, silver-eyed ghoul stood perfectly still. All around him crew members scurried, readying the sound, adjusting the lights, moving equipment into place.

Jake huddled near the door with Mindy and Gregory and a few other extras. "Emory really wants to get this scene filmed," Jake told them. "He's upset because so much time has been wasted."

"I can't believe I'm in a scene with Johnny Scream," a girl said, pressing her hands against her cheeks. "I mean, look at him. He's a *giant*! He's just standing there — and he's totally terrifying!"

Mindy started to say something. But Emory appeared in the doorway, clipboard in hand. His eyes swept the room as he pulled Jake aside.

"Listen, Jake, do me a favor," he whispered.

He really looks tense, Jake thought. I've never seen him like this.

"Don't tell anyone about what happened," Emory said, raising his eyes to the extras at the doorway. "I mean, about the laughing voices, the invisible kids we heard. We don't want to scare anyone — right?"

"Right," Jake agreed. "Don't worry, Emory. I won't say a word."

Emory nodded gratefully. Then he hurried over to the set. "Are we ready?"

Sheila appeared beside him. She turned and motioned to Mindy and the other extras. "Do you know when to come in?" she asked. "When Johnny Scream turns on the power saw, all four of you walk right through here."

"And remember, you don't see him at first," Emory added. "So don't look at him. And don't look at the camera."

Emory talked briefly with the camera operator. Then he had a short conversation on his cell phone.

"Okay, let's try it," he called loudly. "Let's see what this looks like."

The crew members settled into their jobs. Sheila called for quiet.

Jake stood next to his father. He turned and glimpsed Mindy, Gregory, and the others lining up for their entrance.

"Okay, Johnny," Emory instructed. "You toss

back your head and laugh. And then you reach out with both hands and throw the switch on the power saw."

Johnny Scream didn't reply. He stood stiffly facing the saw.

"Ready?" Emory asked.

Johnny didn't move.

"Johnny — ?" Emory called, his voice catching. "Is there a problem?"

No reply. Johnny Scream still didn't move.

"There's something *wrong* with him, Emory!" Jake cried.

"Huh? Wh-what's going on?" Emory demanded, scowling. He shoved his way past two sound recorders and stomped up to Johnny Scream. "Johnny?"

He grabbed Johnny's hand. The curled fingernails came off in Emory's palm.

Emory grabbed Johnny Scream's shoulder. The ghoul's big coat fell open.

Loud gasps rang out through the wood shop.

"Noooo!" Jake screamed.

mpty.

The ghoul's costume was empty.

Emory held the rubber mask in his trembling hands.

Johnny Scream's jacket and tights crumpled to the floor.

"It — it was standing there with no one inside!" Jake gasped.

Shocked cries echoed around the room.

Emory stared at the mask in his hands. Stared . . . his face twisted in horror.

Finally, he turned to Sheila. "Has anyone seen Rad? Has anyone seen Rad today? Who helped him into the costume? Who did his makeup?"

"I — I haven't seen him all morning," the camera operator said. "I thought he was standing there the whole time!"

"Me too," Sheila said, shaking her head. "We all thought he was in his costume."

Emory uttered a nervous laugh and tossed the rubber mask to the floor.

Jake could see that his dad was shaking. He hurried over to him.

"People don't just *vanish*," Emory murmured.

"Emory — let's get out of this school," Jake begged. "This place really is haunted. It's the only explanation."

Emory gazed at him blankly, large beads of sweat running down his pale cheeks.

"Let's get out — please!" Jake pleaded, tugging his dad's sleeve. "Before something even worse happens."

Emory shook his head. "No way!" he boomed. "I'm the King of Horror! I can't let anyone drive me from my own set!"

And then he added in a whisper to Jake, "I can't let them see me scared."

"Emory — please!" Jake cried.

But his dad turned to the crew and boomed, "Set up the final classroom scene. I want to film it this afternoon. *And NOTHING will go wrong!*"

"My dad won't leave," Jake told Mindy after lunch.

"He's very stubborn," Mindy agreed.

"He's frightened. I *know* he is," Jake said.

"He should listen to you," Mindy said softly.

"I hope everything goes okay in the classroom scene," Jake said.

A strange smile spread over Mindy's face. Her green eyes flashed. She didn't reply.

ake knew something was wrong as soon as he and his father entered the classroom.

He saw Emory stiffen. Emory lowered the clipboard to his side. His eyes swept over the brightly lit room.

A shrill hissing sound rose up from the front.

"Sheila?" Emory called, stopping just inside the doorway. "Where is the crew?"

Jake crept up beside Emory and peered into the room.

He didn't see Sheila. And he didn't see any of the other crew members.

The camera stood on its pedestal, the lens aimed into the rows of seats.

The hissing sound grew louder. It rolled from the front of the room back over the room, like an ocean wave.

110

"Sheila? Where are you?" Emory demanded, his voice rising over the shrill hiss. "Where *is* everybody? What is that horrible *sound*?"

"The kids are all in their seats," Jake whispered, moving close to his dad.

"But where is the crew?" Emory asked, swallowing hard.

The shrill hiss forced him to cover his ears.

And then, slowly, the students began turning in their seats.

And as they turned to the back of the room, turned to Emory and Jake, their hideous, twisted faces came into view.

Ghouls.

They were all ghouls. With sagging, melting green skin. Sunken eyes in rotting sockets. Grinning, toothless mouths. Decaying purple tongues lapping at blackened lips.

Chunks of skin fell off their cheeks and chins. Eyeballs plopped wetly onto the desktops and rolled to the floor.

And as the ghouls turned, hissing, hissing as if all the life was leaking out of them — they reached out their arms, yellowed, gnarled, skinless fingers clawing the air as if trying to grab Emory and Jake.

"Nooooo!"

Jake leaped back as a horrified wail burst from his father's throat.

"You're not my actors!" Emory shrieked. "Who

111

are you? Where did you come from? *Where are my actors?*"

The ghouls laughed in reply. Ugly, dry, choking laughter.

Emory uttered another cry as Johnny Scream rose up from a desk. His black lips spread in an openmouthed grin. He lurched to the doorway — and grabbed Emory by the throat.

"You're not Rad!" Emory shrieked, his hands flying up in helpless terror. "You're not the actor!"

"*I'm REAL!*" Johnny Scream declared in an ugly rasp. He tightened his bony-fingered grip on Emory's throat.

"*I'm back from the dead! I'm no actor! I'm REAL!*"

mory uttered a choked cry of protest.

He shot both hands up — and swiped them at Johnny Scream's face. Emory's fingers plunged into the ghoul's doughy green skin.

"Not a mask?" Emory gasped weakly.

And then the rest of the ghouls were on their feet, staggering stiff-legged across the classroom. Hissing . . . hissing . . .

Closing in on Emory and Jake.

Emory pulled free of Johnny Scream's grasp. And fell back against the wall. And opened his mouth in a horrified scream.

"No! Please!" Emory begged as the ghouls closed in. "Please! Please!"

The ghouls froze in place. The hissing stopped.

Johnny Scream took a step back. He lowered his

skeletal hands with their yellow curled nails to his sides.

Emory hunched against the wall, face buried in his hands. Shuddering. His whole body trembling.

"See what it's like?" Jake demanded. Jake couldn't keep a triumphant grin from spreading over his face. "Emory — now you know what it feels like!"

"Huh?" Emory raised his head from his hands.

Jake couldn't hold back any longer. He leaped onto a desk and tossed back his head — and crowed, crowed in victory!

Johnny Scream pulled off his mask. The extras all pulled off their masks. They were laughing hard, laughing and congratulating Jake.

"That's for ruining my birthday party!" Jake told his dad. "That was for trying to terrify me every minute! Now you know that *anyone* can be scared!"

"You mean . . ." Emory shook his head as if trying to shake away his confusion. "You mean you *planned* everything? All the frightening things that happened here?"

Jake nodded happily. "Mindy and Gregory and the other kids helped me. The ideas were all mine. But I couldn't have done it without them."

Emory shook his head again, stunned. "Good work, everyone," he said finally, his voice still trembling and weak. "Good work."

"Admit you were scared," Jake demanded.

"Come on, Emory. Admit it. Admit you were scared."

Emory swallowed noisily. "I was *terrified*," he told Jake.

Later that evening, Jake sat beside Emory in the screening room the crew had set up in the auditorium.

"You really scared me, Jake," he admitted. "But I'm happy about one thing. The camera was rolling the whole time. I got that whole terrifying classroom scene on film."

"Can't wait to see it," Jake said.

Emory turned back to the guy at the projector. "Roll that classroom scene," he called. "Let's take a look."

The lights went out.

The projector clacked to life. Light flickered on the movie screen.

The classroom came into view. Jake gazed at the seats. The desks.

"Where is everyone?" Emory cried.

"They're not there! The classroom is *empty*!" Jake declared.

"But — but —" Emory stammered.

They both stared at the empty classroom.

"They are there. But they didn't photograph," Emory whispered finally. "Ghosts," he murmured. "Mindy, Gregory — all of your friends, Jake. They really are ghosts!"

"Let's get out of here!" Emory declared.

They were in their trailer. Emory began frantically tossing his clothes into a suitcase. "Pack up, Jake. I never want to see this haunted place again!"

"I'll be back in a sec," Jake told him.

He hurried out to thank Mindy and Gregory. "Emory is actually *terrified*!" he told them.

They all laughed and congratulated each other, slapping high fives all around.

"He really believes that you're ghosts!" Jake exclaimed.

More gleeful laughter.

"That film convinced him," Jake told them. "When he saw that no one showed up in the film, he nearly died!"

"We were so clever," Mindy declared. "Whose idea was it to film the empty classroom *before* the extras took their seats?"

"I guess it was mine," Jake said.

"Brilliant! Awesome!" Gregory declared, slapping Jake on the back. "And we never even filmed the kids in the class. Only the empty classroom!"

"So now, thanks to our clever little joke, Emory believes in ghosts," Jake crowed. "You guys have *got* to come visit me in L.A. I can't wait to see Emory's face when you show up!"

They laughed some more. And then said goodbye.

Jake hurried back to his dad in the trailer. As he ran, a final triumphant smile crossed his face.

"Who is the King of Horror?" he asked himself. "Who is the King of Horror?

"*I* am!"

About R.L. Stine

R.L. Stine is the most popular author in America. He is the creator of the *Goosebumps*, *Give Yourself Goosebumps*, *Fear Street*, and *Ghosts of Fear Street* series, among other popular books. He has written over 250 scary novels for kids. Bob lives in New York City with his wife, Jane, teenage son, Matt, and dog, Nadine.